Animal Stories

ISLAND BOOKS

This edition published in 2003 by
S WEBB & SON (Distributors) LTD.
Telford Place, Pentraeth Road, Menai Bridge,
Isle of Anglesey, LL59 5RW

© 1999, 2003 Bookmart Limited

ISBN 1-84322-169-1

Originally published in 1999 by Bookmart Ltd
as four separate titles from the
'*Read with Mummy*' series:
*The Three Billy Goats Gruff, Three Little Pigs,
Puss in Boots* and *The Ugly Duckling*.

Printed in Dubai

Animal Stories

CONTENTS

The Three Billy Goats Gruff

Three billy goats called Gruff live
high on a mountain side.
All day they eat grass and play.

One day, they decide to go in
search of sweeter grass.

They arrive at a bridge across a
river, and on the other side is the
richest, greenest meadow they have
ever seen.

Under the bridge lives a mean old troll who gobbles up anyone who dares to cross.

The first billy goat bravely begins to cross, but the ugly troll hears the *trip trap* of his hooves.

"Don't gobble me up! I am little. My big brother is behind me. Eat him!" "Good idea!" says the greedy troll.

The second billy goat Gruff sees his little brother running about in the juicy meadow.

"I'm not afraid either," he says. He begins to tiptoe across the bridge.

But his hooves make an even louder noise- *Trip Trap Trip Trap!*

Up pops the head of the mean old troll!

"Who's that trip trapping over my bridge?" he roars.

The second billy goat Gruff is very scared.

"Please don't gobble me up, I'm just hair and gristle. My big brother is coming behind me. Why not eat him up instead?"

"Good idea!" says the troll.

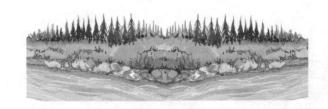

Now the third billy goat Gruff is almost fully grown. He is already quite fat and his horns are long and sharp.

Instead of tiptoeing across the bridge, he begins to stamp across it- THUMP THUMP THUMP!

Up pops the ugly head of the mean old troll! The troll begins to roar.

"Who's that stamping across my bridge?" he roars.

"It's me!" yells the third billy goat Gruff. "I'm very big, juicy and fat. And there's no one behind me!"

The troll climbs from under the bridge.

"Then I'm going to gobble you up!" he roars, and licks his lips.

The troll and the third billy goat Gruff stand at opposite ends of the bridge.

Then they rush at each other!

The troll has big fists but the third billy goat Gruff has big horns.

They meet with a CRASH! and the troll flies from the bridge into the river.

The oldest billy goat Gruff joins his brothers. They look into the deep water. But they cannot see the troll.

Soon the villagers arrive. They are so happy the troll has gone that they start to dance.

And the three billy goats Gruff eat the grass in the meadow and grow very fat indeed!

Three Little Pigs

One day three little pigs wave goodbye to their friends and go in search of an adventure.

The first little pig meets a man with some straw and asks him if he may have some to build a house.

"Certainly little pig," says the man. The first pig builds his straw house and then has a nap.

Nearby lives a wolf. He knocks on the door of the house.
"Little pig, little pig, let me come in!" he calls.

"Not by the hair of my chinny chin chin!" cries the little pig.

But the mean wolf huffs and puffs the straw house down and gobbles up the first little pig.

The second little pig meets a man carrying some wood.

"May I have some wood to build a large house?" the little pig asks.

"Certainly, little pig," says the man.

The second little pig builds a wooden house and then has a nap.

Soon the wolf knocks on his door.

"Little pig, little pig, let come me in!" the wolf calls.

"Not by the hair of my chinny chin chin will I let YOU in!" cries the second little pig.

So the wolf huffs and puffs and HUFFS and PUFFS and the wooden house falls down. He runs inside and eats up the second little pig.

The third little pig meets a man carrying some bricks.

"Please may I have some bricks to build a strong house?" he asks.

"Certainly, little pig," says the man.

The third little pig works late into the night and builds a brick house.

Soon the wolf comes knocking at his door.

"Little pig, little pig, let me come in!" he calls.

"Not by the hair of my chinny chin chin, will I let YOU in!" cries the little pig.

So the wolf huffs and he puffs and he HUFFS and he PUFFS and HUFFS and PUFFS some more. But the brick house will not fall down!

The next day the cross wolf returns.

"Little pig!" the wolf says in his nicest voice. "Let us go and pick apples together in the morning!"

When the wolf arrives the next day the little pig is already up the tree.

"Here!" yells the little pig, and throws a juicy apple at the wolf.

Then he leaps into a barrel and rolls all the way back to his strong, brick house.

The wolf races after the little pig.
He leaps onto the roof of the brick
house.

"I'll get you!" he roars, and climbs
down the chimney into the house.

But the little pig puts a pan of
water on the fire and the wolf lands
in the hot water. He is never seen
again!

And the third little pig lives happily
ever after in his brick house.

Puss in Boots

A poor miller lives with his cat. One day the cat says to the miller, "Buy me a pair of boots and a bag, and I will make our fortune."

The miller is so surprised he spends his last pennies on the cat.

Puss pulls on his boots and catches a large rabbit! Then he slings the bag over his shoulder and goes to the palace.

"I am Puss in Boots!" he tells the King. "I bear you a present from my Lord, the Marquis of Carrabas!"

The King is so shocked by a talking cat that he accepts the gift.

Next, Puss in Boots catches two fat birds and gives them to the King.

"What a kind man this Marquis is." he says, and accepts the gift.

Then Puss in Boots leads the miller
to the river and tells him to go
for a swim.

When the King's carriage passes,
Puss runs into the road.
"Help, robbers have stolen my
Lord's clothes!" he cries.

Soon the miller is dressed in a fine
suit and riding in the
royal carriage.

Puss in Boots runs ahead. He sees some mowers in a lush meadow.

"The King is coming!" he tells them. "You must tell him that this meadow belongs to the Marquis of Carrabas." And he gives them some money.

The King's carriage passes, and the King asks who owns the meadow.

"Our Lord the Marquis of Carrabas owns this fine meadow." The mowers say, bowing deeply.

Now the King is very impressed.

Meanwhile Puss in Boots arrives at the great castle of the nasty ogre.

"Can you *really* turn yourself into an animal?" Puss asks the ogre.

The ogre turns himself into a wild ferocious lion. "Of course," he roars.

Puss leaps on top of a cupboard.

"Do you do small animals as well?" he asks politely.

The ogre turns himself into a teeny tiny mouse.
"Of course," he squeaks.

Puss then gobbles the mouse up!

When the King's carriage arrives at the ogre's castle, Puss in Boots cries, "Welcome to the home of my Lord, the Marquis of Carrabas!"

The King turns to the miller.

"What a splendid fellow you are, you have a clever cat and you bring me presents!" he says.

"Not only that," the king says. "But you own all the best land and you live in the finest castle."

"You are the perfect husband for my daughter!"

So the miller becomes a prince, and lives in the castle with his wife.

As for clever Puss? He hangs up his boots, and lies purring by the fire.

The Ugly Duckling

Mother Duck is very excited. Her eggs are nearly ready to hatch. Soon she will be the mother of six little ducklings.

Her friend says, "One of your eggs is much bigger than the others."

"ALL my little ducklings will be beautiful." sniffs Mother Duck.

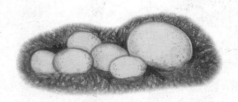

It's time! Five eggs start to crack,
and five fluffy ducklings wriggle out
of their shells.

"Ahhh!" say all the animals.

Then the sixth egg, the BIG egg,
starts to crack. And out steps a very
strange bird.

Mother Duck pretends not to notice
that her sixth baby is a very ugly
duckling indeed.

Mother Duck and her six ducklings go for a swim.
Five little ducklings splash in the water together. But the sixth duckling is too big to play.

"Go away, Ugly Duckling!" cry the other five.

The Ugly Duckling is unhappy. He decides to run away.

But wherever he goes it is the same.

"What a strange bird" cry the geese.
"What an ugly duckling!" cry the
wild ducks.
"Go away!" they cry.

"One day," thinks the Ugly
Duckling, "I'll be beautiful, and
then they'll be sorry." But he does
not believe it.

He is strong and brave. But he is
also lonely, and winter is coming.

He makes himself a home by a lake.

One morning he watches a family of swans flying across the sky.

"How graceful they are!" he thinks. "How happy they must be!"

He sighs. It is getting colder. Snow begins to fall. In the distance the Ugly Duckling can see a farmhouse.

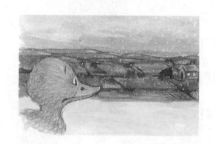

"I wish I lived over there," he thinks to himself.

But he knows they will only laugh at him.

Instead he goes out onto the frozen lake and uses his big feet to skate. He has fun!

The ice melts. Spring has come! The other birds start to arrive back at the lake. The Ugly Duckling hides.

The other birds are too busy to notice the Ugly Duckling. He notices everyone else flying around.

He stretches his wings and suddenly he is flying. "I can fly!" he cries.

He flies past a family of swans. "What a handsome bird!" they cry.

"ME?" asks the Ugly Duckling. He is so surprised, he crashes into the lake.

The Ugly Duckling looks into the water to see his reflection – A snowy white swan is looking back up at him!

"He must be a prince," the swans say. "We would like to be your friend."

"Where do you come from?" they ask.

The Beautiful Swan smiles. "I've been here all the time!" he says.